The
CHAMPION
CHARLIES
The
Grand Finale
D0808923

ADRIAN BECK

Illustrations by **Adele K. Thomas**

RANDOM HOUSE AUSTRALIA

A Random House book
Published by Penguin Random House Australia Pty Ltd
Level 3, 100 Pacific Highway, North Sydney NSW 2060
penguin.com.au

First published by Random House Australia in 2018

Addresses for the Penguin Random House group of companies can be found at global.penguinrandomhouse.com/offices.

A catalogue record for this book is available from the National Library of Australia

ISBN: 978 0 14379 130 0

Cover image and internal illustrations by Adele K. Thomas
Cover design by Tasha Dixon
Internal design and typesetting by Midland Typesetters, Australia
Printed in Australia by Griffin Press, an accredited ISO AS/NZS 14001:2004 Environmental Management System printer

Penguin Random House Australia uses papers that are natural, renewable and recyclable products and made from wood grown in sustainable forests. The logging and manufacturing processes are expected to conform to the environmental regulations of the country of origin.

For everyone who loves
The Beautiful Game

CONTENTS

EXTERMINATE!

It was either JELLY or ANCHOVIES.

Or both.

And Charles 'CJ' Jackson's toes were SQUIRMING in it. The moment he'd kicked off

his sneakers and pulled on his boots – just before the match began – he'd felt the gooey, cold liquid SQUISH through his socks, then up between his toes. Pushed for time, CJ thought he'd be able to ignore it. But late in the second half of the game he still found himself curling up his toes to avoid the STINKY OOZE.

Someone was messing with him. And that someone was in the crowd: Lenny Lincoln. The gorilla with a mohawk. The former Jets captain. The BANE of CJ's existence (apart from maths, of course). Lenny must have snuck the icky mixture inside CJ's boots that morning. CJ often left his football gear strewn about his front yard, so the boots would've been easy to get to. Maybe CJ should've been thankful Lenny hadn't simply stolen them again.

But CJ had to ignore Lenny and his Hammerhead FC mates. NOTHING ELSE MATTERED right now, other than beating the Zenlake Zebras.

‘Stick to the game plan, Jets! If we win today we’re in the Grand Final!’ cried Charlotte, covered in mud and puffing hard in the centre of the pitch. ‘But lose . . . and our season’s over!’

‘Totally, Charlotte!’ yelled CJ, running over to his co-captain, covered in even more mud and looking like some sort of swamp monster. ‘It’s called an *Extermination* Final for a reason, everyone. We need to EXTERMINATE!’

‘Eliminate,’ said Charlotte.

‘Huh?’

‘It’s an *Elimination* Final, dingbat,’ said Charlotte. ‘Leave the details to me, you focus on scoring!’

That was music to CJ’s ears. He didn’t need to be asked twice.

The Jindaberg Primary School football pitch was packed with fans. There were plenty of people in Jets green and gold, but almost as

many in Zebras black and white. Some kids were sitting on the chicken coop for a better view. One was even straddling the old Captain Jindaberg statue's shoulders. The cheering had been as DEAFENING as a crowd at a blockbuster Socceroos match. Even Coach Highpants' booming voice was struggling to cut through the roar. (Just for the record, Highpants was technically named Mr Hyants, but all his students called him Highpants because he wore his pants so high they defied the laws of gravity). The Jets' coach was alongside Principal Swift and the school groundsman, Baldock. Both were blocking their ears as Highpants belted out, 'It's the fiiiiinal count*down*! D'ddle do doo, D'ddle d'do doo!'

This wasn't much help, but Highpants was right. Time WAS running out. There couldn't have been more than a minute on the clock.

The Jets had learned a whole bunch of lessons over the course of their first season

together. They were clicking as a team at just the right time. Everyone was playing their role. From CJ's best mate, Benji, putting his gymnastic skills to good use by setting up unbelievable scoring opportunities in attack, to Lexi in defence, who streamed back to block the opposition just as often as she streamed her viral videos live to YouTube. Even the Paulveriser (real name, Paul) had stepped up his game, guarding the goals almost as fiercely as he guarded his party pies at lunch.

But despite it all, the score was locked at 0–0.

The Zebras were about to throw in the ball on the change rooms' side wing in the Jets' defensive half. Despite puffing hard, everyone got into the right position. Even CJ, who sometimes struggled to follow Charlotte's complicated tactics. After all, CJ sometimes struggled to follow the HOKEY POKEY.

As the Zebra player picked up the ball for the throw-in, Charlotte ran to CJ. 'I hate to say it, but if we're still drawn when the whistle blows, that's pretty much a loss.'

'What are you talking about?'

'I've researched every one of the Zebra players. Backwards,' said Charlotte, gesturing for Antonio to stay on his man. 'Their winger, Penelope, is a TOTAL GUN.'

CJ glanced at Penelope. The girl was cross-eyed, with hair like Einstein and her finger shoved firmly up her nostril.

'*She's* a total gun?'

'They call her Penalty Penelope. Or PP for short. She's never missed a penalty shot,' said Charlotte. 'Unlike me, I'm sorry to say. I've never *scored* one.'

PP put her other finger in her ear and dug out some earwax. She squished it into her frizzy

hair. PP seemed an unlikely threat, but CJ knew better than to doubt Charlotte. His co-captain's preparation was METICULOUS, almost as good as the Matildas coach Alen Stajcic.

The Zebra player took the throw-in. The ball sailed in the direction of a tall Zebra at the top corner of the Jets' box. Lexi flew towards it, her leg at full stretch, but Saanvi was coming from the other side, attempting a header.

KERUUUNCH!

The two Jets COLLIDED into the Zebra, sandwiching him from either side. They all fell to the ground as the ball bounced off them and spilt back towards the centre. All three were left stinging from the clash.

'Ouch!' exclaimed Lexi. 'That better not leave an ugly bruise.'

The collision was a total accident, but the ref blew his whistle. 'Free kick to the Zebras!'

The crowd reacted immediately. Half breathed in sharply, the other half cheered.

The ref placed the ball down a metre outside the corner of the box. Both teams scrambled to get in position for the kick. All the Zebras were in their forward half. They knew this was their LAST CHANCE to score.

'Code Brown!' yelled Charlotte. Her set plays were always inspired by her baby sister, Sofia. CJ didn't want to know what real-life incident CODE BROWN referred to, but at training Charlotte had mentioned something about a bath. EWWW.

'She said, CODE BROWN! Now!' repeated CJ, supporting his co-captain.

The Jets took their places in front of the ball, as the tall Zebras player lined up for the free. Charlotte was busy manning the Zebras' star striker, but as she ran past CJ she pointed to PP lurking further back on the other side of

the pitch. 'If they cross to PP and she shoots, it'll be game over.'

Not if I have anything to do with it, thought CJ. He got himself running before the Zebra even kicked the ball. He THUNDERED towards PP, but he was leaving his man open. If this didn't work out, the Zebras would have a free player to pass to. But risky was CJ's middle name. (Actually, it was EGBERT, but he told people it was RISKY. Wouldn't you?) CJ went for it.

PFFF!

The Zebra took the kick. Sure enough he passed to PP, but CJ had a head start and intercepted the ball.

Suddenly, there was half a field in front of CJ and just the Zebras' keeper between him and the goals. He SPRINTED forwards, the ball at his feet. He heard footsteps behind him. The crowd ROARED. This was his moment!

Everything was a blur, except for the ball and the goals far off in the distance.

He RAN. He BOLTED. He SPRINTED. His legs were pumping FASTER than The Flash.

As CJ reached the top of the Zebras' box, the keeper ran at him. He didn't know if there was time to take him on so CJ HOOFED the ball, just wide of the keeper. It was such a powerful kick his boot came flying off. He slammed into the keeper. They tumbled into a heap just as the ball skidded across the line . . . and INTO THE GOALS!

CJ glimpsed the crowd. The Jets' fans (which did *not* include Lenny and his mates) were all crying out one word: GOOOOOOOOAL!

It was 1–0!

CJ was BUZZING all over! He hadn't even noticed that he and the keeper had both been SHOWERED in anchovies and jelly, thanks to

his missing boot. There was even a little gloopy bit of fish tail that had slivered onto his tongue. CJ couldn't care less, he just gulped it down. SLURP!

The Jets were in the GRAND FINAL!

DID THE PICTURE HIT YA?

'So, *you* put the jelly and anchovies in my boots before the Extermination Final?' asked CJ. He was furiously chewing gum, certain two days later that he could still taste the anchovy chunks that had ended up in his mouth.

Benji laughed. 'Classic prank, huh?'

'Again, it's an *Elimination* Final, dingbat,' muttered Charlotte.

'Is it? Anyway, I'm just glad the squelchy stuff didn't put me off my game,' said CJ, miming his goal for the GAZILLIONTH time. 'What a superstar killer shot, if I do say so myself!'

'You do,' snapped Saanvi. 'And often.'

CJ, Charlotte and all the Jets were waiting in the corner of the school hall during the Monday morning assembly. The rest of the students were sitting cross-legged on the cold, hard floor whilst Principal Swift was using her big owl-like glasses to read off a list of announcements. She was reminding everyone about an upcoming cake stall, but the only student giving the principal their full attention was the Paulveriser. She had him at the word 'cake'.

The large hall echoed Principal Swift's words. It was brick with little windows at the top and, regardless of the weather, it was always freezing inside. Highpants had told the Jets that Swifty wanted to get them up on stage so the whole school could celebrate the exciting news of the team advancing to the Grand Final. Basically, because they were TOTAL LEGENDS. CJ was FINE with that.

CJ gazed at the memorabilia on the wall as he and the Jets waited for their big moment. There was a photo of Lenny. It was among a number of photos of past sports captains, chess champions, debating stars and a pic of Richard 'Spoony' Reeves from Grade Three, who once broke a world record for balancing spoons on his head. Lenny's photo appeared to be staring straight at CJ. He couldn't help imagining Lenny's EVIL chuckle. Sort of like MMWAH-HA-HA-HAAAAA!

But before Lenny's laugh reached ultimate supervillain levels, Principal Swift clapped her hands together and turned to the Jets. 'It's now time to acknowledge the Grade Five football team, our Grand Finalists, the Jindaberg Jets!'

Principal Swift gestured for the Jets to approach and stand alongside her. The group began filing in, as the whole school gawked. CJ made sure he was first and did the double finger **GUN SALUTE**, then blew up his bubblegum till it was the size of a football. Unfortunately, it **POPPED** in his face.

Charlotte walked across the stage steely-eyed, like this sort of attention was never going to distract her. Lexi strode in like she was on the catwalk and even did a bold turn towards the audience that ended with a pout. Once everyone else had shuffled on, Benji cartwheeled in. He got a few claps. That made him grin.

'It's been quite a journey for this young group of footballers. At the start of the season, we almost didn't have a team,' said Principal Swift. 'But this Saturday night the Jindaberg Jets will be travelling uptown to take on the Hammerheads at Hillside's brand-new football pitch, under lights!'

The Hammerheads had finished on top of the ladder, this meant they got to host the Grand Final if they made it through. Which they did. EASY.

'Now, a special mention must go to Mr Hyants, and also to Baldock for their coaching over the course of the season,' said Principal Swift.

Highpants stood up IMMEDIATELY to take an enthusiastic bow, like he was some kind of rockstar. Baldock was nowhere to be seen. Not one for crowds, he was probably working outside somewhere. CJ was glad Baldock got

a mention. He'd done a great job filling in for Highpants at the recent Knockout Cup. Meanwhile, Highpants was gesturing for louder applause and angling for a second bow when Principal Swift continued. 'Please put your hands together – like you mean it now – for the entire Jets team!'

The school clapped. A few whistled. CJ did another GUN FINGER salute.

Principal Swift held up CJ and Charlotte's arms like they were boxers winning a fight. 'I BELIEVE there's nothing stopping them now!'

CRAAAASH!

The hall fell silent.

A photo had fallen off the wall, and the frame shattered as it hit the floor.

CJ was closest. Benji shoved him aside. 'Dude, did the picture hit ya?'

INDABERG JETS

'Nah, I'm cool,' said CJ, noticing it was the photo of Lenny.

Nothing stopping us except for that guy, thought CJ. The ex-Jets captain was sure to bring the Jets back to earth with a THUD.

⚽

The next day, CJ's class was meant to be doing QUIET STUDY in the musty old school library, but Charlotte couldn't contain herself. 'Highpants was hopeless in the Elimination Final,' she whispered. 'He had no tactics, no preparation, no IDEA! All he ever does is sing daggy old pop songs. Where's the proper football advice?'

'Charlotte? Are you feeling okay?' asked CJ, barely able to keep to a whisper, 'You *never* bag teachers! That's my apartment!'

'I think you mean *department*,' sighed Charlotte. They were on the computers, side

by side. Charlotte was deep into some research on past football Grand Finals and CJ was using an app to draw a bum.

Charlotte crossed her arms on the desk then dropped her head into them.

BEEEEEEEEEEEP!

Unfortunately, she was leaning on her keyboard.

She sprang back up. Once everyone stopped staring at her she continued, 'No, CJ, I don't often criticise teachers, but there's a Grand Final on the line! We have every element we need to win, except for a proper coach. Plus, I think I'm getting a cold or something. Does anyone have a tissue?'

CJ started tapping on the mouse. 'Green or orange for the fart cloud?'

'Are you even LISTENING?'

Highpants stood up in the middle of the library. He rotated 360 degrees as he put his finger to his lips. '*Shhhhhhhhhhhhhh!*'

Once Highpants sat back down, Charlotte whispered, 'See, right now Highpants should be reading about football tactics, but check out that book he's got – *Find Your Songbird Within*!'

'Okay, okay,' said CJ. 'What's the big idea then? Who can we get to replace Highpants so close to the game?'

SPLOOOOSH!

Everyone turned to see a mop head splash onto the outside of one of the library windows. It wiped suds about but didn't really clean the grimy surface. Then Baldock's head popped into view. Upon seeing the kids, the craggy old man pulled a face and mumbled to himself.

'Baldock!' exclaimed Charlotte. 'He has some kind of football experience. We learned that at the Knockout Cup. Weren't you going to look into his history?'

'Uh-huh,' said CJ, clicking his fingers. 'I *was* going to do that. But I *hate* boring stuff.'

Charlotte's fingers flew across the keyboard. 'Come on, help out, dingbat!'

CJ sighed. From time to time he had trouble finding the 'B'. He knew it was next to the 'V', but he couldn't find that either. So he SMACKED all the keys at once and hoped for the best.

'What's with all the clicking and clacking over there, Mr Jackson?' asked Highpants, staring down his long nose in CJ's direction.

'Nothing.'

'Right. I'm coming over. I hope to find you're both researching gaseous planets!' said Highpants, as he walked towards CJ.

CJ's bum drawing was still on screen. So he was definitely looking at *something* GASSY. Maybe he could even claim it was a MOON?

Beside him, Charlotte was frantically trying to close all the windows she had open on her screen, each searching for 'Baldock'. But the computer froze and was doing the spinning WHEEL OF DEATH.

Highpants was coming their way. They needed a distraction. CJ noticed the books lined up on the shelf between him and Highpants. He pushed the one on the end. It slapped into the next book. Which slapped into the one after. WHUMP. WHUMP. WHUMP.

DOMINOES!

The books were tumbling into each other, falling flat along the length of the top shelf. The whole class turned to watch. They were bigger books now. Noisier. Everyone flinched as each hardcover book slapped over.

Then the end result of the book dominoes dawned on everyone at once. (Except maybe the Paulveriser). There was a fish tank on the table that sat below the end of the shelf. The last book was about to be sent flying INTO the water. The book in question was a signed copy of Kylie Minogue's biography.

'Noooooooo!' cried Highpants. 'Not Kyles!'

CJ jumped up onto the table in the middle of the room. He DIVED to save the book, but his fingers weren't going to get there.

Fortunately, the Paulveriser's big mitts CAUGHT the book in midair. He'd snapped into 'keeper-mode'.

PHEW.

Highpants rushed over to inspect the book. 'Oh, thank goodness, the Princess of Pop's okay!'

CJ glanced towards Charlotte, but she was gone. *Why had she left in such a hurry?*

Maybe she wanted to get to football training early? Did she expect him to cover for her?

BRRRRRRRRING!

Saved by the bell. Lucky.

As CJ grabbed his bag and headed for the door, Benji pointed out the poster on the noticeboard for the weekend's Grand Final. It read 'GOOD LUCK, JETS!' CJ quickly drew a moustache, a missing tooth and some undies on the Hammerhead cartoon shark.

'Good Luck, Jets'. THEY'D NEED IT. Even with the right coach, CJ still wasn't convinced the Jets could beat the Hammerheads. Jindaberg's arch rivals had improved out of sight as the season went on. Were the Jets headed for BIG TIME Grand Final humiliation?

FOOTBALL FUN FACTS – Famous Finals

- The first ever FIFA World Cup Final was played in 1930 in Montevideo between the two 1928 Olympic finalists, Uruguay and Argentina. Despite trailing 2–1 at half-time, Uruguay claimed a 4–2 victory in front of 93,000 spectators.

- One of the most famous finals in Hyundai A-League history was the 2007 Grand Final, where Archie Thompson scored not 1, not 2 but 5 goals! Melbourne Victory thrashed Adelaide United 6–0.

- The best ever FIFA World Cup Final is said to have occurred in 1970 in Mexico due to the star-studded Brazilian winners. Pelé and Carlos Alberto led their team to a 4–1 victory over Italy, in the first FIFA World Cup broadcast in colour.

- But it was the 1950 FIFA World Cup Final between Uruguay and Brazil that recorded the highest number of spectators – 199,854. Wowsers!

Facts checked and double-checked by Charlotte Alessi.

N.O. NO!

CJ could get used to this.

Despite the threat of rain, a small crowd had gathered at the Jets' training session after school. There were a handful of kids from

CJ's grade and one or two from the other year levels. With a wild grin, CJ took the opportunity to foot juggle for them. Except he was foot juggling his schoolbag.

'The one and only CJ!' announced Benji, as he noticed CJ's antics. 'Most people juggle footballs, but our co-captain can juggle *anything*!'

CJ did a little spin as the bag was in the air, sneaking a glance at the amazed faces looking on. He gave it some hefty kicks.

'But can he beat his record?' wondered Benji, leaning over to CJ. 'What *is* your record?'

'Let's say fifteen,' whispered CJ with a shrug. 'Mile Jedinak's number.'

Benji pretended to count. 'Aaaaand that's number sixteen! A new record!'

CJ **BOOTED** the bag super high. It got stuck in a tree branch above. CJ's pencil case was poking out – his **OPEN** pencil case! Pens, pencils and rulers came **HURTLING** to the ground like falling stalactites. CJ had to use cat-like reflexes to avoid them. He ended up flat on the grass in a star jump pose, with a pointy compass **DANGEROUSLY** close to parts you don't ever want a pointy compass to be dangerously close to. **EEEEEP!**

Checking he still had all his limbs, CJ then burst out laughing. The kids watching clapped in amazement.

Highpants called out from over near the goals, 'There isn't time for you to take a nana nap, Mr Jackson! Get over here! Quick smart!'

CJ jumped up. Laughing, he and Benji joined the rest of the group.

All the Jets were gathered around Highpants. All except Charlotte, who CJ

hadn't seen since she'd left the library earlier. If he stopped to think about it, CJ might have realised something was up, but he rarely stopped to think about anything.

'Children, this is the Grand Final!' said Highpants, his arms praising the sky. 'And yes, the odds are against us. Of course they jolly well are. As I always say, LIFE'S TOUGH!'

Beside CJ, Antonio sneezed and Fahad sniffed. Neither seemed well.

'Not only are we playing the Hammerheads, but we're heading uptown to their brand-new pitch,' said Highpants. 'So make sure you all don't get stuck in an . . . *uptown funk*.'

'Uh-oh,' whispered Lexi.

'He wouldn't,' said Saanvi.

'He *is*,' said CJ, as Highpants revealed a Bruno Mars style pork-pie hat and sunnies,

then began dancing. 'Don't believe me just *watch*! Woo!'

But NO-ONE was watching. Lexi was even shielding her eyes. As Highpants used his long legs to dance, the Jets all took a step back.

'This is RIDICULOUS!'

Everyone spun around. It was Charlotte. She'd dumped her bag on the sidelines and was storming over to the group. Picture the expression on a PIT BULL if someone were to yank on its tail. Well, Charlotte looked ANGRIER.

Upon hearing her, Highpants stopped singing and dancing. For once.

'This is Grand Final week!' said Charlotte, her arms waving about in the air. 'Why are we wasting time singing and dancing?'

Highpants went red and his top lip started sweating. He slipped his hat back into his jacket pocket. If any other student had spoken

to him this way, there would've been a **NUCLEAR** reaction. But Charlotte had always been his favourite. And what she was saying was right.

'I know I'm late. Family emergency or not, there's no excuse. But now I'm here I'm going to make sure we prepare for the Grand Final *properly*!'

'Quite right, Miss Alessi,' said Highpants, shaking his head at the kids. 'Some of the children were getting a little carried away.'

The Jets exchanged glances. They weren't the ones in oversized sunglasses.

'Let's practise something. Come on, chop chop!' declared Highpants. He glared at the nearby football like it was some kind of alien artefact. 'Um, Miss Alessi, I'll leave it to you to make a start. I have a big audition coming up, so I need to squeeze in a spot of vocal practice. Back in a jiffy.'

Charlotte sighed as Highpants danced off from the group. CJ shrugged. The two co-captains got the Jets moving with some dribbling and passing. The team's kicks were precise, their dribbling controlled. The Jets before round one were nothing like today's Jets. A season of hard work was paying off.

'We can beat Lenny and the Hammerheads. I really believe that,' said Charlotte, pumping everyone up.

CJ whispered to Benji, 'I'd like to believe that too.'

'Why not, dude?' said Benji. 'Hey, that'd make a perfect top five.' Benji was a little obsessed with top five lists thanks to the bestseller shelf at his family's newsagency. 'Let me lay it out for you, dude – THE TOP FIVE THINGS THE JETS BELIEVE. (AND NO-ONE CAN TELL THEM NOT TO, SO THERE.)

1) Lexi believes One Direction will get back together. She also believes you can grow EGGS from an EGGPLANT.

2) The Paulveriser believes in a mythical being called the TOOTH-CLAUS-BUNNY. This creature delivers chocolate eggs as presents so he can steal your rotten teeth.

3) Highpants believes his LYCRA cycling outfit looks good on him.

4) I, Benji Nguyen, believe that one day I'll invent a game that's a mixture of Football *and* Acrobatics called FACROBATICS. And . . .

5) CJ, is it still true that you believe because cows say moooo, when they fart it sounds like OOOOM? A *backwards* moooo?'

CJ laughed. 'It's true! I heard one once! I also believe that robotic bums will take over the world one day: bot-bots!'

CJ and Benji cracked each other up. Charlotte tried to ignore them.

Meanwhile, the Jets changed drills. They began practising KICK-OFFS. Then they moved to HEADERS. After that they switched to THROW-INS. If there was ever a movie made based on the Jets – and surely that was just a matter of time – Spielberg would definitely use fast pump up music for this part of the story. Either that or the Chicken Dance (one of CJ's personal fave tunes).

'CJ, you have to agree that all our practice and planning has paid off,' said Charlotte, beside him in line for the drill. 'But there's still one thing missing.'

'Jam donuts?'

Charlotte screwed up her face. 'No, dingbat. Leadership.' She nodded towards the garden behind the Captain Jindaberg statue. Baldock was weeding with his trusty dog, Garlic, by his side.

Charlotte started walking over, gesturing for CJ to join her. 'In the library, before I took off today, I found out a whole heap of info on Baldock.'

'Yeah?'

'He was in all the junior national teams and was on track to play for Australia.'

'Baldock?' asked CJ.

The scruffy old guy was scattering manure on the garden. He wiped his forehead with a grubby hand, which left a brown streak. UNFORTUNATE.

'Yep. But he got injured. Career over,' said Charlotte, and then she tapped her head. 'Bet he still has a football brain though.'

Charlotte led them past the statue. Garlic came bounding up to them. She gave him a quick pat and left him to CJ. After all, the two had a special bond. They both smelt the same,

they both looked like they were allergic to brushes and they probably both had fleas.

Charlotte stood behind Baldock and cleared her throat.

Baldock kept working.

CJ was still patting Garlic a few steps away. The dog was licking peanut butter off CJ's chin. As CJ gave Charlotte an encouraging smile, the dog's tongue slipped in CJ's mouth. EWWW!

Charlotte rolled her eyes. Then she cleared her throat again, louder this time. Nothing. So she tapped Baldock on the shoulder.

Baldock slowly turned around. He was not only the shape of a boulder, but he seemed to move like one too.

'Good afternoon, Baldock,' said Charlotte, like this was somehow more official than talking to a grumpy dude handling cow poo. 'It's the Grand Final this weekend.'

Baldock grunted, then returned to his work. But Charlotte continued, 'We need you to coach us.'

Baldock's craggy face remained blank. CJ wasn't sure he'd even heard what Charlotte had said.

'Um, please?' added Charlotte. 'We know you know football.'

Baldock turned back to his garden and muttered, 'Stinky kids.'

'Hey!' said CJ.

'In fairness you *do* smell like cat vomit today,' whispered Charlotte.

'I do?'

'Yep, an improvement actually,' said Charlotte. 'Get Baldock's attention, go on. Do something stupid. Something CJ-ey.'

As was often the case, CJ did the FIRST THING that entered his mind. He lifted Garlic up and reached out to hold the dog in front of Baldock. Still chewing on peanut butter, Garlic appeared to be talking. CJ did his voice. 'Ruff! Baldock, ruff, fuff! Pweese coach the Jets! It would be ter-ruffic! Ruff-ruff!'

Nearby, Charlotte was cringing.

'Ruff! I wanna sniff someone's butt right now. Ruff, ruff!'

'All right, all right,' said Charlotte, putting a stop to CJ's antics. 'Baldock, we're a good team now, I really believe that. But the Hammerheads have had a PHENOMENAL season. We don't stand a chance without a proper coach. You're the missing piece. Will you at least consider it?'

Baldock continued yanking out weeds. He was strewing dirt everywhere. Charlotte flicked it off her football top like it was kryptonite.

Baldock shook his head.

'Come on, Baldock! Ruff! Rufff-fuff! Do it for your best friend!'

'Pleeeease!' said Charlotte.

The big bulky guy turned around again. He ignored CJ and took a step towards Charlotte. And with his croaky voice he replied, quite simply, 'N.O. NO!'

CJ was starting to get the feeling Baldock was NOT interested in coaching the Jets for their Grand Final.

That was that then. They were stuck with Highpants . . . who was over by the change rooms dancing with a rake.

CHAPTER FOUR

A GORILLA IN THE MIST

Beneath the dark, gathering clouds, Charlotte and CJ returned to the pitch, deflated. Lexi was live streaming on her iPad, commentating on Benji who was channelling his former mascot skills for the growing crowd.

Lexi was pulling so many duckface reactions, CJ half expected her to quack. He missed the days when she just recorded One Direction poems.

A man in a shiny blue suit with a gold tie stepped forward from the crowd. His hair was slicked up to a point. He looked a little like a Troll Doll, but he smelt like he'd fallen into a vat of TOILET SPRAY.

'Mr L is the name – talent scout.' He reached out to shake hands with Lexi and Benji. 'You two kids have got spunk.'

'How rude!' Lexi pouted and then frowned in confusion. 'Hang on. What *is* spunk?'

'The star factor!' said Mr L, as a cheesy grin spread across his face.

Charlotte shot CJ a quizzical look. She seemed MEGA PEEVED at how their training session was panning out. She furiously tightened her ponytail.

'Here's my card. Shiny-hair girl, tiny-acrobat kid, I could make you both stars!' He handed over business cards that seemed to magically appear in his hands. 'You want to excel, call Mr L!'

'Right! That's enough!' said Charlotte, checking her watch. 'I have seven new set plays to teach and just twenty-three minutes before I need to get home and cook dinner. Let's do this!'

As they rejoined the rest of the team, CJ watched Mr L disappear into the crowd. There was something familiar about his hairstyle, but CJ couldn't place it.

Unfortunately, the training session didn't improve. Highpants sung the whole time; Lexi and Benji kept chatting about becoming famous; May, Fahad and Antonio kept sneezing and the Paulveriser's stomach made numerous loud hungry noises. Combined with

the rain that started falling halfway through, it was fair to say that training was a BUST.

This was the first of two sessions the Jets had scheduled for the week. They'd need the next one to improve BIG TIME if they wanted to be ready for the Grand Final.

Developing a bad cough, Charlotte raced home straight after the rest of training was called off, muttering something about AVOIDING ANOTHER FAMILY EMERGENCY.

Benji and Lexi were suddenly great mates, chatting about being 'discovered', so CJ left them to it. The other Jets split off into smaller groups, hurrying home through the misty drizzle that made everything seem spooky. CJ found himself alone at the school gates.

That's where it happened.

THWACK!

A football to the tummy.

'Ooof!' gasped CJ. It knocked the wind out of him. He bent over to catch his breath.

THWACK!

A football to the head.

'Ow!'

Where were they coming from? With the misty rain he couldn't see more than a few metres ahead. CJ covered his face.

THWACK! THWACK! THWACK!

More footballs SMACKED into him. If the first one hadn't caught him off guard he would've tried to use his killer reflexes to swat them away, like Danny Vukovic for Sydney FC throughout the 2016/17 season. But doubled over, CJ wasn't able to defend himself, instead the balls pushed him backwards.

He fell butt first into the school's muddy flowerbed.

SPLOOSH!

The footballs kept coming, but they were missing him now, slamming into the nearby wheelie bins instead.

He thought he heard laughter above, or was it coming from the trees beyond the gate? It was impossible to tell.

'Might as well give up, CJ,' came the voice.

'Lenny?' whispered CJ, wiping mud from his face.

'The Jets don't stand a chance against the Hammerheads!'

THUMP! THUMP! THUMP!

The balls hit the bins again. The smelly contents rattled inside as they wobbled from the impact. More laughs from above.

CJ realised it *wasn't* that the balls were missing him. Whoever was firing off footballs was trying to KNOCK the bins over, on top of him!

THUMP! THUMP! THUMP!

Scrambling to get out of the way, CJ slipped in the mud and fell, knocking over two of the bins. He was unable to get himself upright, and the laughter got louder. There was one bin left standing, and this was the fullest and stinkiest. It began leaning CJ's way, about to spill all over him. One more direct hit and . . .

CLUNK!

A shovel collided with the concrete ground beside the muddy flowerbed. Baldock was holding it, like some sort of wizard's staff. By his feet Garlic barked like crazy.

'Clear off, stinky kids!' growled Baldock.

The laughter went quiet.

'Now!' cried Baldock.

CJ heard rustling in the trees, then footsteps – two or three kids, maybe? – all hurrying away. A voiced trailed off, laughing. 'You'd be mad to believe you can win! The Jets are a joke!'

As he shook the mud from his hair, CJ glanced up at Baldock. He put his hand out for Baldock to help him up. The grumpy groundsman ignored it and grunted. CJ got up on his own.

'Um, thanks for that,' said CJ.

Another grunt.

'Would've got crazy messy.'

'Stoopid,' muttered Baldock. 'Lucky there wasn't glass or somefink in them bins.'

CJ realised Baldock was right. The situation could've gone REAL bad, REAL quick.

'Must've been Lenny Lincoln and his mates,' said CJ, as he and Baldock peered into the mist.

'Brat,' said Baldock.

'Yep. I'd love to show that gorilla and his mates what we're made of on Saturday night.'

'Y'got 'em scared,' said Baldock, rubbing his hairy chin. 'That's why they're 'ere.'

CJ nodded. Maybe that was true. But nodding made his neck ache. He was HURTING ALL OVER.

Baldock looked at CJ and just for a moment his face softened. 'I met ya mum a coupla times, son.'

'Yeah?' said CJ. The funny thing that happens when you lose a parent – which isn't funny at all – is that before long everyone stops mentioning them. But CJ liked hearing about

his mum. He didn't want to pretend as though she never existed. He smiled.

'Nice lady, she was,' said Baldock, flicking a weed from CJ's shoulder. 'Go on. Git home.'

Baldock limped away. CJ pulled his football jumper up over his head to shield himself from the rain and began to run down the street.

The whole way home CJ couldn't shake the thought that the Hammerheads might be right. Maybe the Jets *were* a joke? They'd been thrown together last-minute by Principal Swift. Maybe they'd got by on luck till now. And their prep wasn't exactly going to plan. Were they about to be on the receiving end of a good old-fashioned THRASHING?

FOOTBALL FUN FACTS – Unusual Training

- The superstar striker Luis Suarez always trains with his bootlaces undone. According to former teammate Danny Wilson the Barcelona star never did up his shoes when he was training at Liverpool.
- Super-coach Graham Arnold prefers his team to practice at the same time of day as their next scheduled match. If his team is set to play at night, then they train at night too.
- Technology is changing the way teams train. From professional clubs requiring their players to wear GPS bibs to track their movements, to use of the Footbonaut – cutting edge equipment that encloses a player, then randomly shoots up to 200 balls at them to improve their reflexes. Yikes!

Facts checked and double-checked by Charlotte Alessi.

A PIZZA AND A PENALTY

The misty rain was clearing by the time CJ rounded his street corner. As he slowed to a jog he noticed Charlotte STORMING out of her house. She headed straight to the football that was attached by rope to her totem tennis pole.

She **BOOTED** the ball and it flew around the pole in a blur. In terms of Charlotte's mood, this was **NOT** a good sign. CJ decided to creep past into his house, hopefully undetected.

'CJ!' called Charlotte from across the street.

'Oh, hi. Didn't see you!'

'You took your time getting home.'

'Yeah. Caught up with an old friend,' said CJ, rubbing his tender arms and legs.

Charlotte strode over and gave a defeated sigh. CJ wondered if she was still miffed about their dodgy training session, but then she glanced over her shoulder at her house and shook her head.

'Everything okay?' asked CJ. He didn't usually ask stuff like that and wasn't sure what he'd do with the answer.

'You noticed I had to race home from the library today, right?'

CJ nodded.

'Ronnie emailed,' explained Charlotte.

'What did your little bro want?'

'Mum's got the flu, so Dad's had to take some time off work. But he's a walking disaster zone. Stuffs up *everything* he touches,' said Charlotte, sighing. 'I've demanded he at least cooks the pasta for dinner. It's a *basic* skill. Your dad knows how to cook pasta, right?'

'Knows how to eat it too!' said CJ, patting his belly.

'Hey, are you watching the Sydney Derby tonight? I need to get out of the house. See you for the kick-off?'

'Oh. Erm, sure.'

Charlotte stomped back through her front yard. 'And we can talk tactics for the Grand Final. We need to plan **METICULOUSLY!** Get your brain into gear, okay?'

CJ didn't answer. His brain was in neutral, that's kind of how he liked it. Plus, he wasn't sure what *meticulously* meant, but it sounded super boring.

As CJ tracked mud through his house he noticed his dad, busy in the kitchen. Whatever he was cooking smelt DELICIOUS – it couldn't have been healthy. His dad had always been the cook in their house. CJ began to wonder if maybe that was because he always got to decide what they ate.

'Charles!' said Dad. 'How was school, mate?'

'Good,' said CJ. 'Just one lunchtime detention so far this week.'

'Proud of you, son.'

In fairness, this was a good effort for CJ.

After dinner, his dad retreated to the back room to practice his latest Dancing Dads' routine. Some of the dads at CJ's school were in a dance group. Their routines weren't to everyone's taste (in fact, they were possibly to no-one's taste), but the dads seemed to enjoy themselves.

Minutes before the Sydney Derby kick-off, the doorbell rang and Charlotte burst inside with a pizza box in her hand. Her dad mustn't have been able to master pasta after all. Not one to pass up a second dinner, CJ munched on a slice of capricciosa with Charlotte as the players took their positions on-screen.

Some say the Sydney Derby is more tribal than the Melbourne Derby. It's almost like the whole of Western Sydney gets behind the Wanderers and everyone else is a Sydney FC fan. But CJ was watching for one reason alone: ORIOL RIERA. The Wanderers' goal machine and former roommate of the great Lionel Messi. He's a Spanish superstar that most teams have very little answer for. It was going to be interesting to see what the Sky Blues could throw at him.

The Wanderers took the kick-off. Sure enough, three Sydney FC players broke their formation and headed straight for Riera. This meant he became a decoy and the other Wanderers were able to easily work the ball forward with players free. The ball ended up with the Wanderers' midfielder Kearyn Baccus. He drifted wide, planning to set up a cross. Riera was waiting for the perfect moment.

CJ and Charlotte JUMPED to their feet in the living room. CJ even leaped up onto the couch, accidentally flinging olives off his pizza. 'Riera! Riera's the danger man!'

'But if the Sky Blues stick to their zone – believe in themselves – Riera won't be an issue!' said Charlotte. Then she sneezed. Her cold wasn't getting any better.

As Baccus fired the ball over the top of the box, a Sydney FC defender peeled off his man and collected Riera as the striker charged towards the ball. WHISTLE!

'Look at that! They ended up awarding Riera the penalty!' said Charlotte. 'Should've stuck to their plan!'

The Spaniard striker got to his feet. He ran in and BOOTED the ball, wasting no time converting from the spot kick, low into the bottom-left corner of the goals.

'Niiiiice shot,' said CJ.

'Wish I could do that,' said Charlotte.

'Hey, I saw your booming left foot when you kicked the ball around the totem tennis pole before,' said CJ. 'Lucky you didn't knock yourself out.'

'Yeah, yeah. Right, we need to talk tactics for the Grand Final, if we want any chance of

winning another one of those,' said Charlotte, pointing to the Jets' Grand Final trophy from the boys' team win last year. It was perched on the shelf beside the telly. On the trophy there were some words engraved. The top line was the score and the bottom line said: Leonard Lincoln (C).

Suddenly, the words were **BURNING** into CJ's eyeballs. His former captain was now targeting him. Would CJ be able to believe in the Jets' Grand Final plan, or would he be drawn into a tussle with his arch rival? Lenny had been promising revenge ever since the round one draw. And judging by the afternoon's incident with the footballs, the mud and the bins . . . he was **DETERMINED** to get it.

CHAPTER SIX

SOMETHING FISHY

During Thursday lunch, Charlotte was given permission from Highpants to head home to assist her dad with some sort of garage door malfunction. In the meantime, CJ noticed a professional photographer taking pictures of

Benji and Lexi outside the classroom. Surely the photographer – whoever he was – would want to capture some CJ action too.

'Hey, you want a photo of the Jets' star striker?' asked CJ, jumping up in front of the camera, with TWO THUMBS UP. 'This some sort of publicity for the big Grand Final?'

'The what?' replied the photographer.

'Um, CJ, this is for something else, dude,' said Benji sheepishly.

'It's publicity shots,' said Lexi, striking a pose like it was an everyday thing for her. 'Our new showbiz agent, Mr L, set it up.'

'Dude, I know it's a bit weird,' said Benji. 'But it's also kind of exciting, don't you reckon?'

Before CJ could answer, the photographer shooed him away. CJ spent the rest of lunch defacing the Hammerhead cartoons on the

Grand Final posters that had been plastered around the school.

That afternoon, training wasn't going much better than the previous session. Charlotte was FUMING.

For starters, as the team attempted to complete drills, Highpants was trying on outfits from the local costume shop for the audition he kept mentioning. At first he exited the change rooms dressed in a PINK TUXEDO with a flower print. Then he returned in a PENGUIN SUIT. Then as a GIANT CARROT and last but not least, as a COW with an unfortunately placed udder.

'I can always count on your honest feedback, children,' sneered Highpants.

Benji was the only one appreciating the outfits, mainly because it reminded him of his mascot days.

Highpants went red-faced as Principal Swift stepped onto the pitch. He was now dressed as a CHRISTMAS PUDDING.

'Jets! I do hope your final training session before the big game is going well.' She fixed her big round eyes on Highpants. 'You look . . . festive.'

'Ah, yes,' mumbled Highpants.

'Whatever happens Saturday, I want you all to know that I'm proud of you.'

CJ smiled. Charlotte too.

'You've had a terrific season and . . .' Principal Swift paused and put her hand to her nose. 'I'm sorry, but what's that hideous smell?'

The Jets stared at CJ.

'What?' said CJ, looking a little offended.

But then they noticed Baldock had limped over to the group. The big guy dumped a

BUCKET OF FISH on the ground. Everyone jumped back as the gooey grey and blue creatures gleamed in the sun. He wasn't sure if he was imagining it, but CJ could almost see the stinky fumes floating off them.

'Ewww!' said Lexi.

'Been fishing, Baldock?' asked Highpants.

'Do tell,' said Principal Swift. 'What's the meaning of this?'

'Found 'em hidden all through the change rooms,' said Baldock. 'And someone had also put fish guts in one of the lockers.'

'Gross!'

'Whose locker?' asked Charlotte.

Baldock looked at CJ.

Oh, great, thought CJ.

'Goodness me, who would've done such a thing?' asked Principal Swift.

AUSTRALIA
MATILDAS

CJ knew. And Baldock probably had a fair idea as well.

'It's gone far enough. But never mind all that. Y'want an extra coach, y'got one!' said Baldock. He glanced at Highpants in the pudding costume. 'We'll do it together. Merry Christmas.'

'Woohoo!' cried Charlotte, and she HUGGED Baldock. By the expression on his face he was already beginning to regret his decision.

'Marvellous,' said Principal Swift, kicking off a round of applause. 'And not a minute too soon.'

Baldock got the Jets practising dribbling around Highpants in his pudding costume, then shooting for goal. He didn't say much, but he could grunt and point like no-one's business.

CJ caught Principal Swift smiling as she departed the oval. 'Thank goodness Baldock

agreed to be your co-coach. I would have hidden some fish myself if I'd known that would prove so effective,' said Swifty to CJ. 'I didn't know how many more times I was going to get away with asking Baldock to prune this garden during your practice sessions. There's barely a leaf left!'

The Jets had a new coach. But would it be TOO LATE to help them match it with the Hammerheads?

FOOTBALL FUN FACTS – Great Coaches

- Sir Alex Ferguson is often named the greatest coach/manager of all time. In charge of Manchester United from 1986 to 2013, he's won thirteen Premier League titles. That's more than any other football coach in history. Wowsers.
- The coach who has won the most Hyundai A-League Championships is tied four ways. As of 2018, Kevin Muscat (Melbourne Victory), Ernie Merrick (Melbourne Victory), Ange Postecoglou (Brisbane Roar) and Graham Arnold (Sydney FC) had each won two.
- The first coach to take Australia to the World Cup finals was Rale Rasic in 1974. The Aussies managed two losses and a draw. In 2004, Rasic was awarded the Medal of the Order of Australia (OAM) for his service to football.

Facts checked and double-checked by Charlotte Alessi.

CHAPTER SEVEN

A NOT-SO-EARLY NIGHT

Baldock didn't muck around. He was super strict. There was **NO** slacking off, **NO** distractions and **NO DAGGY POP SONGS**. Baldock had the Jets training almost as professionally as the Socceroos. He was a real do-er, communicating pretty much in grunts alone.

Best of all, Baldock kept Highpants under control. 'I'll just duck off to get changed out of my Christmas costume and do a few vocal warm-ups.'

Baldock didn't even glance over at him. 'You aint goin' nowhere, puddin'.'

Halfway through the session, CJ was panting beside Charlotte as they waited for their turn to practise a corner kick. 'I've never trained so hard in all my life!'

Charlotte grinned. 'Great, isn't it!'

She took off to receive the corner kick. CJ gave chase. It *was* great. This was just what they needed. But coming this late in the process, would it be enough to take them to the next level?

At Friday lunchtime, Baldock held an extra training session. All about tactics. Charlotte

was in **HEAVEN!** She handed out a stack of papers with all her research. Highpants turned up too, but his suggestions were often delivered in the form of a song and were ignored by Baldock.

It turned out Baldock knew more of the Jets' set plays than some of CJ and Charlotte's actual teammates. Certainly more than the Paulveriser, who remembered two set plays at best. Perhaps the info had seeped in during all that time spent gardening while the Jets trained. Baldock's football experience and Charlotte's carefully calculated ideas were the **PERFECT COMBINATION**. CJ could see why Charlotte had been desperate to find a 'proper' coach. It was the missing ingredient.

The only thing that made it difficult to concentrate was the sniffing, sneezing and coughing that the group were doing throughout the session. But CJ was pretty sure they'd all be 100 per cent by the next day.

By the end of lunch, the whole team was prepped and ready to go for tomorrow's BIG GAME. Except Benji and Lexi who hadn't shown up.

CJ asked Charlotte what had happened to them. She flared her nostrils as she explained they had the afternoon off school because they were recording a video 'screen test' for Mr L.

'Well, that's just unpredictable,' said CJ with a huff.

'I think you mean *unacceptable*. And I agree,' said Charlotte. Lexi was sure to cop an earful the next time she saw Charlotte.

As the Jets left school for the day, Baldock waited by the gate and grunted, 'Get some sleep, stinky kids.'

Baldock was right. On the night before a Grand Final, the SMART thing to do was to go to bed early. But CJ wasn't smart. Besides, he knew he'd never be able to sleep, so he swung by Benji's family newsagency to see if his best mate might be there. There was a ripping W-League game on that night and he wondered if Benji and his dad, Mr Nguyen, might be keen to head along. CJ found his friend bringing in the newspaper headline stands that leaned against the shop's front window.

'Hi, mate!' said CJ. But Benji was practising some kind of speech and barely noticed.

'Earth to Benji?'

'Oh, hey dude,' said Benji. 'Just practising my lines for tomorrow.'

'Tomorrow?'

'Yeah, Lexi and I are doing a football socks commercial for the internet.'

'You serious? Socks? That *sucks*!' said CJ. 'You do realise we've got the Grand Final tomorrow, right?'

'Yeah, but we'll be done in plenty of time,' said Benji, immediately looking guilty. 'The Grand Final's at night, remember.'

CJ glanced at Benji for a moment. Then he laughed. Benji wouldn't let the team down. He told himself to stop stressing, he was becoming Charlotte. GROSS!

'No worries, mate. Hey, there's a ripper game on tonight, you keen?'

AAMI Park was teeming with people as CJ and Benji battled to keep up with Mr Nguyen who was powering ahead. Melbourne City were taking on Perth Glory. Or Kyah Simon vs Sam Kerr. With Kerr playing – one of his all-time

favourite players – CJ was barracking for Perth all the way.

'Dude, don't forget about Steph Catley. She might just give Kerr a hard time tonight,' said Benji. 'Which leaves Kyah Simon to do some damage!'

'Yeah, yeah,' said CJ.

They found their seats on the wing and CJ took a moment to soak it all in. Under the lights the stadium was even more spectacular than during the day. The atmosphere at a night game was SOMETHING ELSE. And tomorrow he'd be playing under lights too, for the first time, at the Hammerheads' new pitch.

It was just minutes into the first half when Kyah Simon took charge. City were thundering down the field with Glory on the back foot. Simon had the ball on the far side of the pitch. She DANCED around two defenders, then back-heeled the football to Sofia Sakalis.

'Check this out, check this out!' cried CJ, standing in his seat.

Sakalis weaved through traffic then chipped the ball back to Simon at the top of the box. Using the momentum of the ball, Simon gave it the slightest nudge and the ball SKIDDED off into the bottom corner of the goals.

GOAL!

Despite going for Perth, CJ leaped from his seat. Benji Laughed. 'Hope you're taking notes, dude. We don't want to have to wait for another late goal to save us from penalties.'

'Relax! It's all coming together now! Nothing can stop us!' replied CJ. He glanced around at the celebrations in the crowd. Everyone in the stand opposite was jumping up and down as one. SUPER PUMPED. Everyone except the kid sitting dead centre. When CJ saw him, he was certain something in his brain popped. CJ could no longer hear the crowd's

celebrations. The kid was staring straight back at CJ. The kid had a mohawk and his muscles bulged through his T-shirt. It was LENNY! They locked eyes. Lenny started to grin. He looked a little like the Joker.

Then someone's drink sprayed onto CJ and Benji. For a moment they ducked for cover. The crowd noise was back. CJ glanced across the pitch to where Lenny had been, but he was nowhere to be seen.

One thing was for certain though. CJ would see him tomorrow.

CHAPTER EIGHT

SHET OR JARK?

CJ had hardly slept.

Every time he closed his eyes he saw Lenny grinning at him, among the cheering crowd in the grandstand. Even when CJ started

counting sheep, soon enough all their heads had mohawks.

As CJ got stuck into a mountain of cocoa flakes for breakfast, he realised he still had the whole day to kill. That was the problem with a night Grand Final. He wanted to be at the pitch already.

Looking for trouble, CJ stepped outside. And he found it. Charlotte THREW open her door across the street and stormed out of her house. CJ could tell she was fuming – even by Charlotte's standards – so he ducked behind the pot plants on his doorstep.

'I'm sorry, dear!' called Charlotte's dad, from inside the house. He was poking his nose through a little window; the dunny, CJ figured. 'But unblocking toilets is just not my strong suit!'

'Well, I can't do *everything*!' replied Charlotte. She put her hand to her mouth,

seeming shocked by what she had just said. CJ wondered if she'd ever admitted such a thing before in her life.

Some clunking noises sounded from inside her house. And suddenly . . . GUSHING.

'*Ma va la!* It's BROWN!' cried her father through the window. 'Ahhh! And lumpy! Someone make it STOP!'

Charlotte reached down to a little pipe gizmo sticking out of the ground near the wall and turned off the water at the mains.

'*Meno male!* Oh, thank heavens!' exclaimed her father. Although, his voice sounded rather muffled. Probably best not to think about why.

Charlotte booted her football around the totem pole. She thumped it once one way, then the other, then she jumped sideways in the air and SMACKED it with all her might. The football

ripped clean off its rope. It hurtled through the air towards CJ. He ducked further down behind the pot plants.

KERRRASH!

He hid is face. The pots SHATTERED above him. He was showered in broken bits of pot, dirt and plants. CJ paused in a crouched position, just to ensure the explosion was over.

Charlotte sighed. 'You can come out now, CJ.'

'Oh, hi Charlotte.' CJ popped up with a daisy on his head. 'Didn't see you there.'

'Sorry about that,' said Charlotte. 'It's just the Grand Final, plus Dad has got me all wound up.'

'Really? You?' laughed CJ. 'By the way, what are you doing for the rest of the day?'

'Arguing with my dad, I reckon.'

'I've got a better idea.'

Using his dad's ancient VHS technology, CJ had tapes of A-League season highlights, the Socceroos' World Cup games and the Matildas' final match at the Rio Olympics. He and Charlotte sat down to watch a football marathon. The perfect build-up!

During the Matildas' penalty decider in Rio, Charlotte turned to CJ. 'WORST NIGHTMARE. They needed their own Penalty Penelope out there.'

'In our team, I'm the PP,' declared CJ.

Charlotte laughed. 'You heard what you said then, right? You're the peepee?'

CJ threw a cushion at her.

Late in the afternoon, it was time for CJ's dad to drive him uptown to Hillside. After waiting

all arvo for the moment to come, now it felt like everything was happening ALL TOO FAST.

As they pulled into the car park, the sky had gone a dark purple. 'This the place, son?'

'I think so,' said CJ. He couldn't help but stare. It was like a MINI STADIUM, with six towering lights that soared into the air like magical beacons. Shiny new grandstands stood proudly beneath. There was a sign all lit up at the busy entrance, 'Hillside Park – home of the Hammerheads.' And there was a statue of a shark with evil eyes and frightening teeth. (Much cooler than the Captain Jindaberg statue at the Jets' pitch). The shark looked a lot like Lenny. CJ made a promise to himself that he'd draw a moustache on it one day.

CJ spotted Antonio and Saanvi. As the three of them gathered under the giant shark, they all seemed to gulp at once. Then Saanvi sneezed.

'Just dust! That's all!' said Saanvi. 'I'm not sick! Promise!'

Inside, everything was silver and new, reflecting the bright moon that hung low in the sky. The stands were already filling up. There was plenty of black and blue Hammerheads colours, but CJ was glad to spot a bit of green and gold dotted here and there as well.

CJ couldn't see any Hammerheads players, but he could hear them. The noise of a team yelling and pumping each other up was spilling from the change rooms. Their pre-game routine seemed well underway.

Baldock was waiting outside the visitors' change rooms. He had an ill-fitting suit jacket on but still wore his overalls and boots underneath. He grunted to call them over.

Charlotte was inside. She was using the brand-new smartboard to sketch out some

set plays. The benches were all padded, the lockers had electronic locks and the whole room had that new car smell.

May, Fahad and the Paulveriser entered. The Paulveriser had a pie in his hands. Actually, the pie was all over his hands and on his chin. 'Good pies here.' He BELCHED.

Charlotte lowered her eyebrows. 'Don't give yourself indigestion before the game, Paul.'

'You have your routine, I have mine.' He shoved the remainder of the pie into his mouth, topped off with a squirt from his packet of sauce.

There was no sign of Benji or Lexi.

As if reading CJ's mind, Charlotte checked her watch. She sighed.

CJ tried to do something to take her mind off it. So he started writing one of Benji's top five lists on the whiteboard. He managed the title: THE TOP FIVE WAYS JINDABERG IS BETTER THAN HILLSIDE – but CJ wasn't as good as his best friend at that sort of thing. Plus, he got distracted by Highpants' bag sitting alongside some of the team's gear. There were various costume items sticking out. Usually by now, the team would have had to sit through five dodgy pop ballads.

'Righto, gather round, stinkies!' said Baldock.

Music started playing outside. Dance music. The lights all went different colours. Then the crowd cheered.

'Pre-match entertainment,' explained Charlotte. 'Don't get distracted.'

That was easier said than done. The song that was playing was the same tune CJ's dad had been practising to all week.

'Surely not . . .' muttered CJ, as he ran to the door.

Out on the pitch THE DANCING DADS were starting their routine. They were all smiles, under lights with a big crowd clapping them on.

'I gotta feeling!' A live voice sung out through the speakers. A familiar voice. 'That tonight's gonna be a good night!'

Then CJ saw who was singing: Highpants! He was striding down an aisle of the grandstand, a mic in one hand, his other arm outstretched. He was dressed as a Jet plane on one side and a Hammerhead shark on the other. A Shet or a Jark?

CJ now knew what their coach had been auditioning for, and it looked like he got the gig. Highpants jumped from the steps and onto the pitch and joined The Dancing Dads for a QUICK BLAST of dance moves.

Somehow The Dancing Dads group had just got even SCARIER.

'Stop watching that and listen,' said Charlotte, blowing her nose.

'Gladly,' muttered CJ, who suddenly noticed his throat was scratchy.

It was difficult to hear Baldock's words with all the coughing and spluttering in the room. As the instructions continued, Antonio had to lie down with a hot towel on his forehead. Saanvi was going through tissues by the box. And May was sneezing little mucus explosions.

'Don't get too close to our star keeper,' said Charlotte, noticing May was sneezing all over the Paulveriser.

'Me?' said the Paulveriser with an upturned lip. 'Nah, I don't get sick.'

After putting their fists together for a 'Gooooo Jets!' the team all ran out onto the field. Those that could anyway. They were a couple of players down. One or two stayed in the change rooms, furiously sucking on oranges to try to perk themselves up.

Plus, Lexi and Benji were still a **NO SHOW**.

On the Hammerheads' side there was just one player missing. CJ glanced around, trying to spot Lenny. Could he have got the flu as well? Could they be that **LUCKY?** But just as the ref blew her whistle to indicate the game was about to start, the last Hammerhead hit the pitch. The crowd roared. He lined up to take the kick-off.

LENNY. CJ's arch rival. The Lex Luthor to his Superman, the Darth Vader to his Luke Skywalker, the pineapple to his pizza.

Lenny's hair was **TALLER** than ever. His **MUSCLES** seemed like they were barely contained by his skin. And his grin twisted across his

face like he was **PART DRAGON**. The guy made an impression, that's for sure.

Lenny didn't pass to any of his teammates. The moment the whistle sounded he just thumped the ball straight into CJ's tummy. Just like the kick CJ had received a few nights back in the mist after training.

'Ooof.'

'Welcome to the Grand Final, CJ,' snarled Lenny. 'Or in your case, it'll be a *Grand Finale*.'

FOOTBALL FUN FACTS – Rivalries

- Cristiano Ronaldo vs Lionel Messi: the two greatest footballers in the world right now also happen to play on teams (Real Madrid and Barcelona) that have a fierce rivalry. Can you choose your fave?

- Socceroos vs New Zealand and Japan: the Aussies have a healthy rivalry with the Kiwis in all sports, including football. But the rivalry with Japan began at the 2006 World Cup, where the two countries were grouped together and have since had oodles of hard fought battles.

- Diego Maradona vs Pelé: they didn't play in the same generation but are probably the two best footballers ever. This causes huge rivalry between fans of the two. Is Pelé the best of all time? He's won three World Cups with Brazil, to Maradona's one with Argentina.

Facts checked and double-checked by Charlotte Alessi.

FINALS FEVER

Grand Finale.

CJ didn't speak French, but he got the idea. Lenny was trying to spook him. And it was working.

With CJ doubled over, Lenny ran onto the ball and passed off to a kid with a shaved head. His Hammerheads teammates called him Nude-Nut. He was as bald as Kevin Muscat. Maybe his lack of hair meant less wind drag, because he sped past a snotty Antonio and soon there was only sneezy May between Nude-Nut and the Paulveriser in goals.

May ran at the guy. He feinted left, but she was onto him. With the lights gleaming on his scalp, Nude-Nut nudged the ball off to Lenny. The ball looked like a tiny marble when big Lenny had it.

'You're the only Jet I still like, mate!' shouted Lenny to the Paulveriser. 'But don't think that's gonna stop me.'

As he approached the goals, Lenny HOOFED the ball high. The Paulveriser leaped, but he merely brushed the underside of the ball with his fingertips. It flew over the top of the Jets' keeper and SLAMMED into the net.

Lenny launched straight into his gorilla celebrations. But this time round, he ran past CJ and mimed picking nits out of CJ's hair to eat.

'That's more common in monkeys, not gorillas, Leonard!' called Charlotte, always a stickler for the facts.

The Hammerhead captain wasn't fussed. All his teammates piled on top of him to celebrate. The grandstands were going wild. This was the **WORST POSSIBLE START** for the Jets. Over on the sidelines, Baldock kicked a garbage bin and Highpants started singing, 'The only way is up!'

Baldock grunted at him to keep quiet.

As CJ got in position for the Jets' kick-off, Lenny stared him down. 'I owed you that, CJ. And there's plenty more coming.'

Charlotte shook her head at CJ. 'Don't get distracted by him, we need to stick to our plan. We need to *believe*.'

But what good was all that when the Jets were five players down?

Baldock was grumbling something over on the sidelines, but CJ couldn't tell what he was saying. Highpants started arguing with him. Great. That's all the Jets needed.

The ref blew her whistle and CJ blindly passed the football wide to Saanvi, but she wasn't there! Huh? She was covering for Lexi in defence.

Lenny ran onto the ball. He laughed at the top of his voice and took a long shot at goals. The crowd GASPED as it almost got past the Paulveriser again.

'Drop back, Jets! Dirty Bib!' yelled Charlotte, referring to their set play titled 'DIRTY BIB'. 'Full defensive mode. NOW! Nothing gets past us!'

The Jets formed a zone defence. But with not enough players there were plenty of gaps.

CJ could see a **HUNDRED** different ways the Hammerheads might break through and score. He just hoped the Jets were strong enough to make it to half-time. Maybe then their other players would be well enough to get on the pitch.

CJ spotted Principal Swift up in the stands with some of the other Jindaberg teachers. She had a green-and-gold beanie on, plus a scarf and possibly even pipe cleaners or something woven around her big round glasses.

It occurred to CJ that if it wasn't for his principal's idea to combine the girls and boys teams at the start of the season, he wouldn't have had a football season at all, let alone be playing in a Grand Final.

'I'm trying not to let you down, Swifty,' muttered CJ. Right then she looked at him. She gave him a little nod and continued chatting with her colleagues. Coincidence? Not usually with Swifty.

The next five plays in the match were all Hammerheads. Lenny linked up with their speedy strikers and set himself up for shot after shot on goal. But the Paulveriser knew Lenny. Even if he didn't realise it (and let's face it, he didn't), instinctively the Paulveriser was able to read Lenny's moves. So far, he'd saved **EVERYTHING** since Lenny's first shot. The Jets were surviving and maybe they might just make it to half-time.

As the ball was retrieved for a throw-in, CJ turned to the Paulveriser. 'Keep it up!'

The Paulveriser sneezed. An explosion of snot burst from his nose and he groaned, 'Don't feel too good.'

CJ's stomach dropped. The team were already **DECIMATED**. If they lost the Paulveriser to illness as well, then the Jets were done for. This was all going horribly wrong. Maybe Lenny was right: the Jets were a joke.

A SMASH AND A RASH

Minutes before half-time, Lenny got the ball past CJ in the Hammerheads' defensive half with a little flick out wide. Like the rest of the team, CJ had been run off his feet. He was starting to get sloppy. That was DANGEROUS. That's when you concede goals.

Never once considering defeat, CJ gave chase, but Lenny had more than a metre on him. The guy's massive tree-trunk thighs were working overtime.

'Dude, I've got him!'

Dude? CJ wondered to himself. The voice came from downfield.

CJ glanced up, it was Benji. He was in his Jets kit, straight off the bench.

'Am I glad to see you!' called CJ.

Benji ran at Lenny and held him up. CJ approached from behind. Lenny was forced to loop the ball up and over Benji. It was headed for the top of the box – a RISKY spot, but LEXI was in the gap. She mopped up the ball and sent it to Charlotte in the centre. Charlotte passed out to Antonio on the wing, unfortunately he was having a coughing fit and a Hammerheads player beat him to the ball.

As they tussled for possession the ball was knocked out of play.

'Where have you guys been?' asked CJ.

'The sock commercial filming was a big scam,' said Benji. 'Mr L, right? The L stands for Lincoln. It was Lenny's uncle. He's a legit talent scout, but there was no real ad to film.'

'So it was camouflage?' asked CJ, as Charlotte joined them.

'Do you mean *sabotage*?' suggested Charlotte.

'Erm, maybe,' said CJ, glancing at Lenny, who was preening his mohawk for the photographer on the sidelines from the local paper. 'I knew that agent's tall hairdo was familiar. Super sneaky.'

'Yep. Once I worked it out we asked to leave,' said Benji.

'But O.M.Jeepers, the taxi took super long to arrive,' complained Lexi.

‘Not sure they ordered one, Lex,’ explained Benji. ‘In the end we decided to run here!’

CJ grinned and gave Benji a high five. Then he turned to Lexi with his hand up.

‘Don’t touch me, sweaty boy,’ said Lexi.

The ref blew her whistle. HALF-TIME.

The Jets filed back into the change rooms. The crowd cheered both teams off the pitch. Once inside, everyone – except Benji and Lexi – seemed to collapse. Sneezing and coughing echoed through the room. It was like the start of one of those movies where a super-virus causes the END OF THE WORLD. And in some ways, it would feel like the end of the world if the Jets lost the Grand Final.

Just as Baldock was about to speak, Charlotte’s mum, Mrs Alessi, barged in. ‘Hello, dears!’

'Mum, you're supposed to be home resting!' said Charlotte.

Mrs Alessi looked pale and had puffy red eyes, but even when she was sick she still had a smile that could light up a room. She carried three thermos flasks in a basket. She placed them on one of the benches.

'Just dropping off a little something your father and I have been cooking up,' said Mrs Alessi. 'Chicken soup for you all!'

Then Mrs Alessi glanced at CJ. 'Your mum's recipe, young CJ.'

Baldock mumbled something in the corner as the team got stuck into the soup. Highpants was singing some old rock song, 'Wooooah, we're halfway there.'

Before Highpants could belt out the next line, Baldock **SHOVED** a pair of footy socks

into his mouth. He spat them out and started waving his finger at Baldock.

Unable to stop herself sniffing, Charlotte worked the room, pumping up her teammates. CJ started doing the same thing as he handed out soup. He took a sip himself. The stuff was SUPER TASTY. It made him think of winter nights in front of the fire with his mum. In a way, it was like she was with him now.

Then CJ noticed the whiteboard. Benji had finished off the top five list that CJ started.

THE TOP FIVE WAYS JINDABERG IS BETTER THAN HILLSIDE.

1) There's no-one at Hillside Primary who can slice a banana with their unusually long big TOENAIL. Nice one, CJ!

2) Even if bot-bots do take over the world, at least Jindaberg students will be able to survive on eggs from the chickens.

3) Jindaberg Primary would definitely have WAAAAAY more cases of nits than Hillside. (Go on, scratch. You know you want to!)

4) They don't have a world record-holder at Hillside! Go Spoony!

5) Unlike here, the school statue at Jindaberg is NOT wearing a pair of BRIGHT YELLOW UNDERPANTS.

'What? Hang on.' CJ began laughing. 'Did you put undies on their shark statue?'

'I put Charlotte's brother, Ronnie, up to it the moment we arrived. Classic!'

Then Principal Swift entered the room. 'Yoo-hoo! Just checking on my favourite team! Go Jets!' She waved the end of her scarf.

'We need a word.' Highpants took Principal Swift aside. They stood with Baldock, but the

three adults were still close enough for CJ to hear. 'Ms Swift, this co-coaching arrangement is not working.'

Baldock didn't argue.

'You need to make one of us the proper coach,' demanded Highpants.

'I will do no such thing. Gentlemen, you're both adults, I'm sure you can work this out,' said Principal Swift, as though she was talking to bickering Grade Ones. 'Baldock has the football IQ and you, Mr Hyants, have the big booming voice. I would've thought you'd make the perfect combination. And I expect to see it in action.'

Highpants' mouth opened and closed like a GOLDFISH for a second or two. Baldock just grunted.

With that, Principal Swift cheered, 'Go Jets!' and left the room.

The soup was MASSIVELY popular. Almost all of it was gone. It was certainly making CJ's throat feel better.

'Gather round, children,' announced Highpants. 'Your co-coaches have some important tips for the second half.'

Highpants turned to Baldock and whispered, 'What are they again?'

Minutes later the Jets burst back out onto the pitch. CJ felt like he was playing in a brand-new team. They had the right numbers and the soup had pepped everyone up. Even though she wasn't here anymore, his mum still knew how to save the day! Hopefully it would be enough. All the elements were in place, but did CJ truly BELIEVE the Jets could win?

CJ took the ball and plonked it in the centre. Charlotte called out instructions. Highpants did the same thing but not in the form of a song. For once he was giving helpful advice.

CJ suspected 99.9999 per cent of it came from Baldock.

Charlotte ran over to CJ as the Hammerheads took their positions. 'Let's try NAPPY RASH. I've noticed the Hammerheads are slow to man-up.'

Baldock nodded from the sidelines. Beside him, Highpants called out, 'We agree. Time for Nappy Rash! I think I heard that right. I want NAPPY RASH, CHILDREN!'

The Jets were all on the same strange page.

CJ FIRED off the ball to Charlotte. She passed all the way back to the Paulveriser. Every other Jet ran to the centre.

'Now!' yelled Charlotte.

Each Jets player started sprinting. Just like Nappy Rash, they spread out from the centre. The Paulveriser BOOTED the ball and Benji took it at his feet, then dished it off to Lexi.

Getting around the Nude-Nut, Lexi nudged the ball to CJ.

Lenny ran at him. 'Come on, CJ, see if you can take on a *real* captain!'

CJ kept the ball moving side-to-side at his feet, but he wasn't gaining any distance.

'Teach me a lesson, mate!' jeered Lenny.

CJ **REALLY** wanted to. But that wasn't the final step in the **NAPPY RASH** set play. But did he care? It would be the best thing ever to dribble past Lenny and boot the ball into the back of the net right in front of him.

No, he couldn't get distracted. He had to believe in the plan. He had to trust his team. So he flicked the ball to Charlotte. She took a millisecond to steady and she **THUMPED** the ball. The football soared between two Hammerhead defenders and towards the lower corner of the goals. It was one of those shots that

looked perfect right off the boot. The mainly Hammerhead crowd behind the goals fell dead silent as they watched the ball.

But the keeper got his hand to it. That wasn't part of NAPPY RASH!

The ball bounced off the keeper. It flew up into the air. There was no time to think – CJ wasn't big on that anyway. He leaped into the air. CJ THUMPED his forehead into the ball. It sailed straight over the keeper who was still on the ground.

GOAL!

It wasn't pretty, but it counted.

1–1.

They were all tied up at Hillside Park! Just like the first game of the year. CJ made sure he ran past the grandstand to celebrate. Principal Swift was on her feet cheering. CJ got to the

corner flag, spun around it and landed on his side. Then came the STACKS ON.

The Jets could beat these guys, CJ could feel it! NOW, he believed!

But as the second half continued the score didn't change. The Hammerheads tightened up their defence and the Jets kept up the pressure. Neither team gave in.

Then came the full-time whistle.

'The match is drawn. 1–1,' declared the ref. And then she spoke the words Charlotte was dreading. 'The Grand Final result will be decided by a penalty shootout.'

FOOTBALL FUN FACTS – Penalties

- In 2017, Sydney FC took out the Hyundai A-League Championship against Melbourne Victory after Danny Vukovic starred in a penalty shootout at Allianz Stadium. Before then, Vukovic had lost three Hyundai A-League Grand Finals.

- A year earlier in the 2016 Rio Olympics, the superstar known simply as Neymar scored the winning penalty. Hosts Brazil beat Germany 5–4 to win their first men's Olympic football gold medal.

- Also in the 2016 Olympics, the Matildas lost their quarter-final to Brazil after a penalty shootout that ended up 7–6. Our keeper, Lydia Williams, stood tall, but Tamires booted the winner that Alanna Kennedy couldn't match. It was a real heartbreaker.

Facts checked and double-checked by Charlotte Alessi.

SICK KICKS

Charlotte and CJ gathered the Jets in the centre circle. Nearby, Lenny had his team huddled together too. They were all grinning around him, like HYENAS about to go hunting.

Highpants began striding over to the Jets, but Baldock grabbed him by the sleeve. At the same time the ref blew her whistle, officially ensuring Highpants remained on the sidelines. Coaches had to stay out of it. Those were the rules of a penalty shootout. It was ALL up to the Jets.

'Right, best of five,' said Charlotte. 'We need to choose five kickers.'

'Me and four others,' said CJ, with a cheeky nod.

'Well, yeah. Okay,' agreed Charlotte.

Meanwhile, the ref nominated which goals both teams would be kicking towards. It was the end with all the Hammerhead supporters. *Great*.

CJ glanced over at the Paulveriser. He was rubbing his nose and his eyes looked like they were getting redder and redder. Despite the soup, he was getting SICKER by the SECOND.

Benji put his hand up.

'Mate, who are you waving at?' asked CJ.

'I'll take a penalty kick.'

'Oh,' said CJ. His best mate would **NEVER** have volunteered for something like this at the start of the season. Benji used to be all about pranks and silly dance moves. He would've run a mile from something this serious. CJ nodded. 'You're in.'

Charlotte was scanning her eyes over the group. The Jets looked exhausted. They were sick and they were nervous. 'Lexi,' she said. 'You've got a powerful left foot. Wanna put it to the test?'

'If someone films it for me,' replied Lexi.

'Think your dad's got that covered up in the stands,' said CJ, giving Mr Li a thumbs up. He was with the other Dancing Dads, filming the scene with an iPad.

'Right, we need three more,' said CJ.

'Two more,' corrected Charlotte. Maths had never been CJ's thing.

'What about you, Saanvi?' asked CJ. 'You're always super accurate.'

CJ and Saanvi didn't get along at school. But what did that matter? On the field they were teammates through and through. She nodded. And seemed a little surprised that CJ had chosen her.

That left just one more kicker.

Baldock was grunting from the sidelines. He started pulling at the back of his hair. Like he was trying to give himself a new HAIRDO.

'Oh for heaven's sake, children, he's asking for Charlotte. The man's pulling his hair into a ponytail!' yelled Highpants. 'Baldock wants Miss Alessi to be the last kicker.'

Charlotte's face went white and she smiled nervously. She looked like she'd rather jump into a BULL RING with a TARGET painted on her BUTT than put her hand up to take one of the spot kicks. After all, a GRAND FINAL result was on the line.

She glanced over at Baldock. He raised his chubby little finger and pointed it straight at her.

'I agree, Charlotte,' said CJ. 'We should have both our captains in the mix. Let's finish off the season together.'

Charlotte took a deep breath and stepped over to join the kickers. 'I'm warning you, I'm no PP.'

'Enough talk of PP. I should've used the toilet at half-time,' replied CJ, shifting his weight on his feet.

The ref blew her whistle. Lenny won the coin toss and decided the Hammerheads would kick first.

Nude-Nut left the centre circle to take the first kick. The home crowd CHEERED as the kid marched forwards. The Paulveriser, coughing and spluttering, took his position in the goals.

For the first time ever, CJ felt sorry for the big guy. If the Paulveriser didn't manage to stop enough goals under the bright lights of this over-the-top stadium, in front of a full house of rabid Hillside fans, the Jets would lose the Grand Final. EPIC FAIL.

The Paulveriser rubbed his nose as Nude-Nut sized up his kick. The crowd's cheering died down. Everyone could sense the moment.

Charlotte put her hands to her face, almost covering her eyes. Benji danced on the spot. CJ jogged around the Jets' group unable to contain his nerves.

Nude-Nut ran in and **BOOTED** the ball. It sailed high and right. The Paulveriser picked it. He'd anticipated the kick and leaped into the air. But the Paulveriser had a very low centre of gravity. He didn't manage to get far enough off the ground. The ball **SAILED** into the top corner of the goals and the Paulveriser **SLAMMED** into the ground. The Hammerheads erupted!

The ref signalled a goal, but no-one could hear her over the crowd.

Nude-Nut took a little bow as he returned to the centre.

'Who's up first?' asked Saanvi.

'Don't look at me,' said Charlotte.

'Well, they call me the *finisher*,' said CJ.

'Who does, dude?' asked Benji with a grin. 'They might call me the *starter* after this!'

Benji confidently jogged towards the penalty spot. The Hammerheads' goalie had swapped with the Paulveriser and was crouched over, alert, waiting in position.

The crowd fell silent again. CJ shivered as he felt the chill in the night air. His best mate used to be the team's mascot, pulling wacky manoeuvres and singing silly songs. But right now he was the MOST IMPORTANT player on the pitch.

Benji stepped back from the ball. He turned to CJ and winked. 'This'll be a classic.'

CJ ducked behind Charlotte, almost too nervous to watch.

Sensing the tension, Benji took a deep breath. Then – from a standing start – he cartwheeled in, forward flipped and finished with a single cartwheel back towards the Jets. As he spun through the air his foot SMACKED into the ball.

The Hammerheads' goalie stood, open-mouthed, gaping at Benji's antics. By the time he realised the penalty kick had been taken, the ball was ALREADY well on its way. The keeper dived for it, but he was too late. The ball skidded over the line.

GOOOOOOAL!

The shootout score was 1–1.

The Jets celebrated as one in the centre. Yelling, hugging and high-fiving. Benji ran back to them and got among it. SNOT FLEW EVERYWHERE.

'Great stuff, Benji!' exclaimed Charlotte.

'Classic!' said CJ. 'As you would say!'

The next Hammerhead strode out from the circle. Lenny patted him on the back as he headed for the penalty spot.

The Paulveriser wandered back to the goals, coughing as he went. CJ wondered if their

keeper might actually COLLAPSE before this was through.

The Hammerhead took a long run-up. He BOLTED in and SMASHED the ball towards the goals.

The Paulveriser was too busy coughing to move, he didn't budge an inch. But the ball went STRAIGHT to him. The Hammerhead was anticipating the Paulveriser would dive, just like the last time. It was a NO GOAL!

CJ shook Charlotte by the shoulders with excitement. She snuck to the back of the group. 'Cover me if I throw up.'

'If you want me to take the next kick, I will, Charlotte,' said Saanvi.

Charlotte nodded.

Saanvi jogged to the penalty box to take her shot. The Hammerheads' goalie was in position so Saanvi wasted no time. She THUMPED the

ball low and left. But the goalie dived. He got a fingertip to it. The ball was knocked into the post and bounced back into play rather than across the line.

'Ooooooh,' cried the crowd.

Saanvi hung her head.

'Great effort!' encouraged CJ. 'Super close. Still 1–1.'

The Hammerheads' next kicker approached the ball. CJ expected Lenny to have taken a shot by now, but the big buy was biding his time.

The Paulveriser managed to stare straight ahead for a moment. Just long enough for the Hammerhead to take her kick. The Paulveriser let himself collapse to the right and . . . STOPPED the goal!

'Nice one. Here's our chance to edge in front!' said CJ.

Lexi was next to take a shot. Standing beside the ball she waved to the crowd. A few even waved back. She blew a kiss to the iPad in her dad's hands, then turned and blew one to the Hammerheads' goalie. He immediately went bright red and, right at that moment, Lexi unleashed an almighty THUMP on the ball. It sailed low and quick towards the goals. The Hammerhead goalie dived. But it was coming SO FAST it just grazed his fingers.

GOAL!

'You better have recorded that, Dad!' yelled Lexi, as she gave a dazzling smile to the crowd.

After three kicks, the score was 2–1 to the Jets! The Hammerheads would have to get at least one more goal to draw the shootout and keep their chances alive. But Charlotte and CJ still had their kicks to take. If they both scored the Jets would WIN the Grand Final. It all came down to the co-captains. The so-called CHAMPION CHARLIES.

THE WINNER IS...

Charlotte used her big brain to do the maths one more time. 'It's 2–1. Both teams have two more chances to score. We can still lose this!'

'And we can still win this!' said CJ. 'We're one goal up!'

Charlotte was so wired, her hair was almost STANDING ON END. Then her eyes went wide. CJ realised why: Lenny. The Hammerheads' captain was heading for the penalty spot. He intended to tie it up: 2–2.

As he strode towards the ball, Lenny glanced back at CJ. He THUMPED his chest like a gorilla. The whole stadium saw it. They all copied.

THUMP! THUMP! THUMP!

They got faster and faster.

CJ glanced over to the Paulveriser. The Jets' goalie looked like a ZOMBIE. Actually, he made zombies look good – he was puffed up, dripping with sweat and super snotty. There was NO WAY he'd be able to stop any more shots. Lenny was about to make minced meat of him. The crowd's chest thumping sped up as Lenny THUNDERED towards the ball.

The Paulveriser **SNEEZED**. This wasn't your average sneeze – his **WHOLE HULKING BODY** sneezed. And with it came a **MASSIVE** dollop of **SNOT**. It flew forwards, not quite all the way to Lenny but close enough to make him flinch. Lenny pulled his kick and the ball went **STRAIGHT UP** in the air!

'Noooooo!' bawled Lenny. He dropped to the ground.

The crowd stopped thumping their chests. They went quiet.

CJ couldn't contain himself. It was bad form to yell and scream, but he couldn't stop himself **JUMPING** on the spot.

'Well done, Paul!' cried Charlotte.

The Paulveriser wiped his hand on his face, clearly not 100 per cent sure of what just happened. He wandered out of the goals a little dazed and confused.

'We get this, we go two up,' said Charlotte. 'They can't catch us. We win!'

'I know,' said CJ, stretching out his leg as he imagined SCORING the winning penalty. Once again the incredible Charles 'CJ' Jackson was about to SAVE THE DAY!

Charlotte was pacing around. 'We just need one good kick. Just. One. Good. Kick!'

The crowd murmured. They'd figured out the sums too. They all knew that a Jets goal meant GAME OVER.

'Believe!' sung Highpants from the sidelines.

CJ shot his coach a FILTHY look. More singing was the last thing they needed right now. CJ was using the precious seconds to visualise his winning kick. He gestured to Baldock to quieten Highpants down. But Baldock patted Highpants on the back to encourage him. It almost seemed like Baldock put him up to it.

'If we miss this kick, we let them back in with a chance!' said Charlotte.

CJ turned to Charlotte as she spoke. He saw the FIRE in her eyes. She wanted this just as much as he did.

'Then don't miss,' said CJ, his arm out, gesturing towards the ball that waited on the penalty spot.

'Me?'

CJ nodded. 'I believe.'

Charlotte gave him a little grin. Then she turned and slowly exited the centre circle. 'This could be the Matildas in Rio all over again. Heartbreaking.'

'No chance,' said CJ.

She strode to the position. She was DETERMINED to make this count. PENALTIES SHMENALTIES. This was the Charlotte CJ knew.

Charlotte glanced at the goals. She sized up the Hammerheads' goalie. She eyed off the ball.

All the lights seemed to be trained on Charlotte and a sudden silence came over the stadium. She ran in.

With her ponytail horizontal, Charlotte ROCKETED towards the ball. The goalie was up on his haunches. With every step, grass flew off her boots. The run-in took just seconds, but it also seemed to last a lifetime.

Right at the ball, Charlotte swung her leg with FULL FORCE. She thumped the ball with ALL HER MIGHT.

SMACK!

The football flew like a missile as it POWERED through the cold night air.

But the goalie saved it! He caught it, right in the bread basket!

CJ dropped his head. All Charlotte's fears had come true. **AND** this meant the Hammerheads could still pinch a victory.

The ref blew her whistle and called out, '**GOAL TO THE JETS!**'

'What?' CJ looked up. The Hammerheads' goalie had been pushed **ACROSS** the line as he caught the ball. Charlotte had kicked the football with such force that the keeper had moved into the goals, taking the ball with him.

There was another whistle, quietening the crowd. 'The Jindaberg Jets are the winners of the Grand Final!' the ref declared.

And after that it was a **TOTAL BLUR**.

Charlotte ran over to the Jets. There were teammates' faces, all **DELIGHTED**, jumping about everywhere on the pitch. Baldock and Highpants were there. Water was being **SPRAYED** over **EVERYONE** and somewhere beyond their

cheering, the Jindaberg school song started playing over the speakers. CJ felt **ON TOP OF THE WORLD!**

THE JETS HAD JUST WON THE GRAND FINAL!

CHAPTER THIRTEEN

THE CHAMPIONS

Soon after the game, a presentation area with a little stage was set up on the pitch. Each of the Jets was asked to come up and receive their individual medal. Principal Swift was handing them out. She waited till last to call out CJ and Charlotte's names. They ran up to Swifty and

she **HUGGED** them before putting medals round their necks.

CJ did a little dance on the spot, Charlotte couldn't help laughing. Then CJ grabbed the mic. He could feel everyone around him step closer to stop him.

'Relax! I just want to say –'

'Thanks to all the supporters that came along tonight,' said Charlotte, butting in.

There was a cheer.

'Yes, that,' said CJ. 'And –'

'And to the Hillside Hammerheads,' interrupted Charlotte, again. 'For putting up such a good fight.'

'Well, yes,' agreed CJ. He glanced over at the Hammerheads. Some were lying flat on their backs while others gawped at the ground. Lenny was looking anywhere but at CJ.

'Anyway, last of all I'd like to thank *me*!' said CJ, pointing at himself.

'And the whole Jets team!' suggested Charlotte.

'Yeah, all right. Come on up!'

The Jets ran back on stage. Amidst the cheering and dancing the Jets were presented with the trophy. Unlike the A-League Champions trophy, CJ was relieved to find this one DIDN'T look like a toilet seat. The entire Jets team, including Highpants, Baldock and even Principal Swift, were all crammed on the little stand as green and gold confetti was shot into the air and the Jindaberg school song played once more.

As Lenny and the Hammerheads left the Jets to celebrate – including a less than perfect performance of 'We Are The Champions' by Highpants and The Dancing Dads – CJ got

CHAMPIONS

Lenny's attention. He ran over to him offering to shake hands.

Lenny stared at CJ's hand. He took it. 'You're not a *terrible* captain, I guess. We'll see, next season.' Lenny SQUEEZED his hand so hard, CJ had to shake himself free.

Then the photographer from the local paper called CJ over to join Charlotte.

'So *you're* Charlotte and *you're* Charles? Do you both get called *Charlie*? I've got a great idea for a headline!' The photographer gestured to the sky, as if the words were appearing above them: 'The . . . Champion . . . Charlies.'

The guy looked at CJ and Charlotte wide-eyed. This was the exact same headline that had been printed last year after the Grand Finals, when CJ top scored for the boys' team and Charlotte captained the girls.

'No, I don't like that headline,' said Charlotte. 'It's not really accurate.'

'Huh?' said CJ. 'I know *I'm* a champion. And you're not bad yourself. Seems right to me.'

'No. It's not just about you and me,' said Charlotte, nodding over at the rest of the Jets celebrating nearby. 'It's about all of us.'

CJ grinned. She was right. They were all in this TOGETHER. Every element 'clicked', from Baldock to the Paulveriser. That's why they were able to win.

'Mr Photographer-guy?' said Charlotte. 'Please leave off the Charlies bit. Just call us The Champions!'

⚽

The next day Principal Swift held a barbecue for THE CHAMPIONS and their families up on the Jindaberg Primary football pitch.

There were green and gold streamers draped from the big old tree, to the Captain Jindaberg statue, to the chicken coop, through the playground and finishing at the change rooms. The school football pitch was nowhere near as shiny and new as the Hillside pitch, but it felt like home.

There were balloons everywhere and a cake that read 'CONGRATS TO THE JETS THEN UNDERNEATH FOOTBALL CHAMPIONS'. Charlotte pointed out to CJ that the 'then underneath' bit was a mistake, but CJ didn't get why.

Mr and Mrs Alessi manned the barbecue. Mrs Alessi seemed to be a hundred times healthier than the day before. She wore her usual smile as she checked on the lamb chops, fish in foil and burgers. Beside her, short little Mr Alessi was turning a few snags.

'Oh no, is your dad going to burn all the sausages?' laughed CJ.

'You know what, I think they'll be okay,' said Charlotte, grinning at her father who was wearing an oversized 'kiss the cook' apron. 'He was just out of practice around the house. But now his work hours are changing and he'll be home more, he might be handy to have around.'

'Cool,' said CJ. And he noticed for the first time ever that Charlotte had her hair out. She wasn't even wearing her watch. Something was going on with her, but CJ couldn't quite put his finger on it.

Near the change rooms, Highpants, Baldock and Principal Swift were each munching on a sausage. They were laughing, retelling the highlights from the night before. Even Baldock had a little grin.

'This calls for a song!' announced Highpants to everyone on the pitch.

But Baldock **SHOVED** a sausage into Highpants' mouth.

Benji, Lexi, the Paulveriser and the rest of the Jets were booting the football around. There were still a few sniffles among the group, but most looked like they were feeling better. CJ got involved, he started re-enacting his Grand Final goal, with commentary and all, but Saanvi angrily stole the ball.

'Fine,' grumbled CJ.

'Dude, we did it!' said Benji. 'Can you believe we're the champions?'

'I knew you had it in you,' said CJ.

'You did not!' said Charlotte.

'Well, I do now!'

After checking and double-checking her hair, Lexi started filming everyone. She spoke to the camera, 'Hello out there! This is the best group EVEEEEER!' She paused, then she thought about it before continuing. 'Actually, second best group to One Direction!'

'Didn't they break up?' asked Charlotte.

'This is the best group EVEEEEER!' proclaimed Lexi again.

In the meantime, the Paulveriser had thumped the football into the cherry blossom tree and now it was stuck.

CJ climbed up onto the monkey bars and balanced on top. Under his arm he had the seat of the swing with the chains stretched out horizontally from the swing's frame. He had that wild CJ look in his eye.

'Come one! Come all!' announced Benji. 'Watch CJ attempt another dangerous dare.'

'I'm going to leap onto this swing, fly over the top of the statue, then I'll BICYCLE KICK in midair – Wayne Rooney style – and boot that football right outta the tree!' declared CJ. 'And I'll have to be quick before Swifty notices what I'm up to!'

Charlotte shook her head. 'That old statue is in your path, CJ. You found that out the hard way last time.'

CJ glanced at the statue. He thought about it for a moment. 'You're right, Charlotte. I'll be sensible.'

'Good. Get down,' said Charlotte, relieved. 'Glad to see you're finally learning your lessons.'

The Jets started heading for the barbecue.

'Here I go!' cried CJ, as he put one foot on the seat of the swing.

Charlotte, Lexi and the others turned back around. Just in time to catch CJ pushing himself off. He started swinging. FAST. His hair whooshed straight. 'Woohoo!'

SMACK! BANG! CRASH!

'Oooof!'

READ ALL THE BOOKS IN THE CHAMPION CHARLIES SERIES

Read on for an extract from the first book in the series

The Champion Charlies: The Mix-Up

SMACK, BANG, CRASH!

The Champion Charlies.

That was the ACTUAL front-page headline on the local newspaper. In big CAPITAL letters. Right beside a 'free burger' coupon.

The page had been plastered onto the school clubroom's noticeboard since last year. The noticeboard was on the outside wall that faced the football pitch. By now the whole school had seen the article. Charles 'CJ' Jackson and Charlotte Alessi were posed in their Jets FC football gear for the photo. The shot was taken after their Grand Finals. CJ's team had just won their match in a nailbiting finish. Whilst Charlotte's team had thumped their opposition to claim the title in the girls' league. They were all smiles. They were CHAMPIONS! They were being peed on by a dog.

'Garlic!' laughed Benji Nguyen, as he exited the clubrooms and patted the kelpie on his way past. 'Your aim is worse than your breath! Get outta here, boy!'

Garlic jumped from the bench and ran off to find his owner, the school gardener, Baldock.

Benji had found what he was looking for in the clubrooms. A megaphone. Holding onto his signature Socceroos cap, Benji sprinted towards the playground beside the clubrooms where CJ was grinning maniacally on top of the monkey bars. CJ and Benji were best friends, both TOP OF THEIR FIELD. CJ was the Jets' leading goalscorer and Benji was the Jets' leading mascot. And also the *only* mascot. Not just for the Jets, but pretty much for the whole Under 11 boys' league.

Below CJ, Charlotte stood beneath the monkey bars with her arms firmly crossed. She ALWAYS wore her hair in a neat no-nonsense ponytail, but right now CJ thought her hair was pulled back tighter than ever.

'This is so NOT funny, CJ,' said Charlotte. 'If you end up in hospital, you won't be able to go to the big Matildas match with us on Thursday night!'

'Hospital! Yeah right,' said CJ with a snort.

Lexi Li had the school iPad out, videoing the whole scene, selfie-style. Lexi was the closest thing Charlotte, who could be pretty uptight, had to a bestie. As Lexi hit record, she flicked her fringe so that it cascaded perfectly over her big dark eyes. She was destined to become Insta-famous one day. Somehow she even made the Jindaberg Primary School uniform look good. Lexi moved from the football pitch to the playground, to the school chicken coop, unable to stand still. 'CJ, let me find some good lighting. If this goes viral I need to be looking my best, okay?'

CJ was balancing on top of the monkey bars. His scruffy blond hair battered by the wind. He'd whacked the seat of the swing under his arm and carried it up there till the chains stretched out horizontally from the swing's frame. There was a wild look in his eyes.

Even more so than usual. Like he'd just eaten a whole pack of Tim Tams.

The kids' football was stuck in the blooming cherry blossom tree. And the school lunch break had only just begun.

CRISIS!

'Stop wasting my time, CJ. I've allocated exactly twenty minutes to football, twenty minutes to writing a book report and twenty minutes to knitting my little sister a green and gold beanie for Thursday,' said Charlotte, checking her watch as she so often did. 'Clearly, the sensible, and *safer*, thing to do is just ask a teacher for help. Not do *whatever* you're planning. You dingbat!'

'I take that as a compliment!' giggled CJ. Then he lost his balance. He flung his free arm about to steady himself. As he regained his footing he only laughed louder. 'Relax! I've got this!'

'Come one! Come all!' announced Benji, as he finally worked out how to switch on the megaphone. His voice echoed down the slope from the football pitch to the rest of the school below. 'Watch CJ attempt another dangerous dare . . . will he fly like an eagle, or will he go the way of the dodo. Either way, you don't want to miss it!'

Charlotte shook her head at Benji as more and more kids ran over.

'Sorry, Charlotte, this is just too good to ignore,' laughed Benji. They may have all been in the same class but they didn't all share the same sense of humour. 'Gather round, catch CJ in action so you can say you saw him when he still had his teeth!'

'Get down, CJ!' snapped Charlotte. 'That old statue is in your path anyway. We can just throw a tennis ball at the football. That might knock it free.'

‘Chill, Charlotte. I’ve got this sussed,’ said CJ, rubbing his hands together. ‘I’m going to leap onto this swing, fly through the air so high that I miss the statue of that old dude –’

Charlotte glared at CJ. ‘Captain Jonas Jindaberg, who our home suburb is actually named after. Show some respect!’

‘Yep, right over old J-Berg’s head, then I’ll bicycle kick in midair – like Wayne Rooney against Man City in 2011 – and boot that football right outta the tree. Game on! Simple!’

‘You’ll never clear the statue,’ huffed Charlotte.

‘Will so.’

‘Will not,’ said Charlotte, turning to Lexi. ‘I kind of want you to keep filming this just to teach him a lesson, okay?’

Lexi looked away from the iPad to give Charlotte a thumbs up, then returned to pulling her best duck face.

Benji put his mascot moves to good use and cartwheeled beneath the monkey bars. 'Give me a C! Give me a J! What does it spell?'

'Nothing they're just initials,' said Charlotte.

'Oh yeah,' said Benji.

'Are they? I thought his name was French or something,' admitted Lexi, still smiling for the camera. Lexi and her father won a Daddy/Daughter beauty contest when she was just three, before the family left New Zealand. Ever since, she could bust out a cheesy grin in mere nanoseconds.

CJ glanced at the crumbly concrete statue. The dude was some sort of olden days ship captain. He was looking skyward, barking orders. CJ HATED following orders.

'Here I go!' cried CJ, as he put one foot on the seat of the swing. Then he pushed himself off. He started swinging. Fast. His hair whooshed straight. 'SEE YA, SUCKERS!'

The swing flew low. CJ shifted his weight, ready to somersault. About to try to bicycle kick the ball from the tree. He swung higher, and higher and then . . .

SMACK! BANG! CRASH!

CJ hit the statue. He squished right into it. Then hung onto it like it was his long lost teddy bear.

'Ouch!' cried Benji. 'I'll always remember that nose as it was, before it was shattered into a thousand pieces.'

The swing kept swinging without CJ. It smacked into the overhanging tree, and then pulled on the branch as it swung back down. The branch split off the tree and started hurtling towards the statue. CJ squeezed his eyes shut.

KERAAACK!

The broken end got lodged straight down the throat of the statue.

'That's got to clear the sinuses, folks!' cried Benji.

It looked like the statue was SPEWING OUT blossom. A huge explosion of colour was being hurled right out of old J-Berg's open gob.

'You know what? You were right, Charlotte,' grinned CJ, as he peeled his face free. 'I was never going to clear this statue.'

Charlotte shook her head.

'What on earth is going on up here?' cried Principal Swift, as she arrived on the pitch, glaring at CJ through her big round glasses that made her look like an owl.

The scene spoke for itself: kids gathered around CJ who was hugging a SPEWING STATUE. It was not a good look.

Charlotte spoke up. 'We were trying to retrieve the football, but –'

'But CJ took things too far?' asked Principal Swift, her big eyes bore into CJ's soul.

'It was a classic!' laughed Benji.

'Sorry. I was just super keen to play football,' said CJ. 'The season starts this weekend.'

'No it does *not*,' said Principal Swift, shaking her head at the state of the statue.

'What?' asked Charlotte.

'You heard. And this goes for both teams. This year, there'll be no football!' said Principal Swift, as she turned sharply and stormed back down to her office.

Despite all the pain CJ was in, it was Principal Swift's words that hurt the most.

NO FOOTBALL!